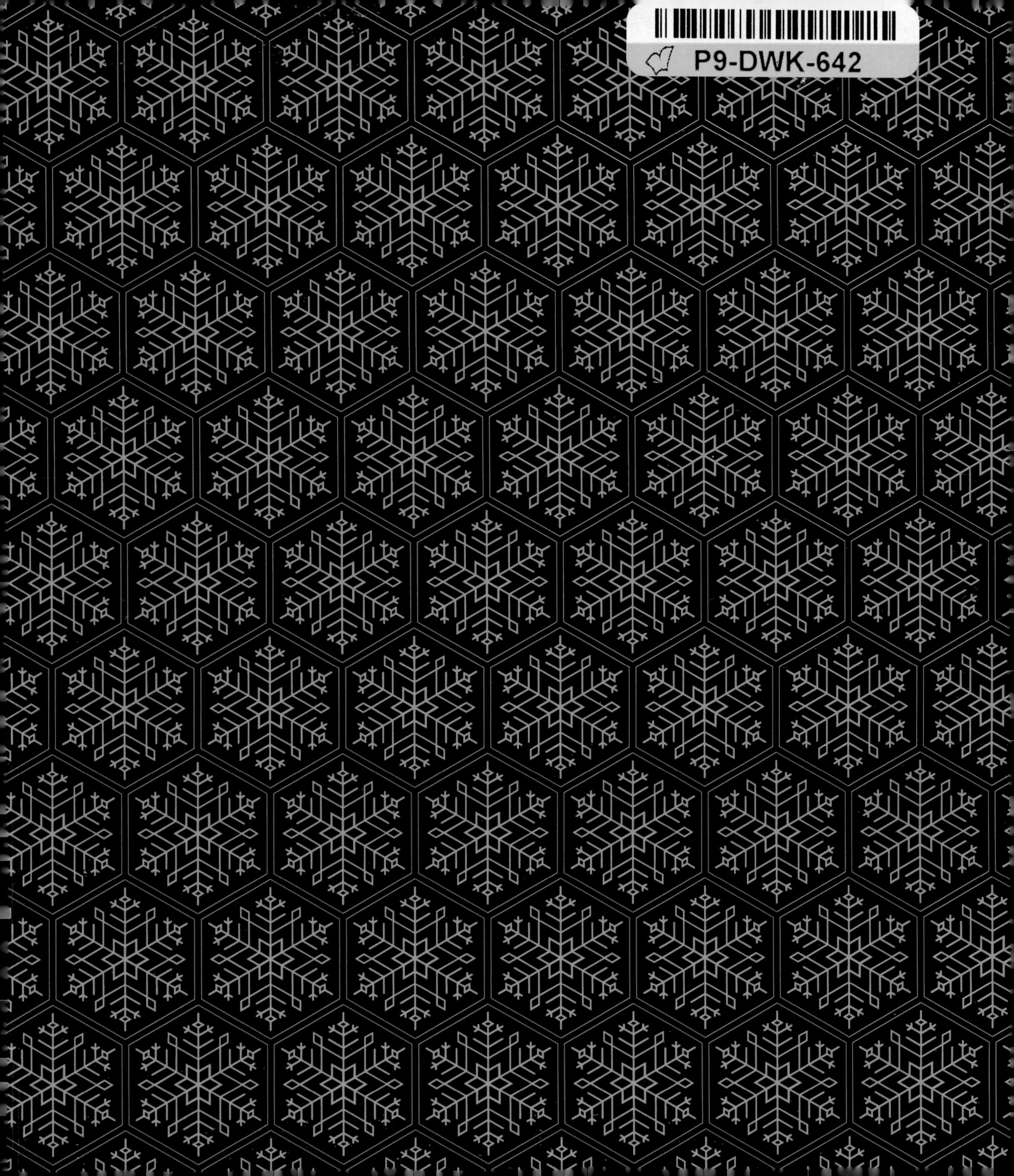

Christmas Tales

Christmas Tales

Celebrated Authors on the Magic of the Season

with photographs by Steve Lovi

VIKING STUDIO BOOKS
Published by the Penguin Group
Viking Penguin, a division of Penguin Books USA Inc., 375 Hudson Street,
New York, New York 10014, U.S.A.
Penguin Books Ltd, 27 Wrights Lane, London W8 5TZ, England
Penguin Books Australia Ltd, Ringwood, Victoria, Australia
Penguin Books Canada Ltd, 10 Alcorn Avenue, Suite 300,
Toronto, Ontario, Canada M4V 3B2
Penguin Books (N.Z.) Ltd, 182–190 Wairau Road, Auckland 10, New Zealand
Penguin Books Ltd, Registered Offices: Harmondsworth, Middlesex, England
First published in 1991 by Viking Penguin, a division of Penguin Books USA Inc.

1 3 5 7 9 10 8 6 4 2

Grateful acknowledgment is made for permission to reprint the following copyrighted works:
"Crisp New Bills for Mr. Teagle" by Frank Sullivan from *The New Yorker*. © 1935, 1963 The New Yorker Magazine, Inc. Reprinted by permission.
"My Christmas Carol" by Budd Schulberg. Copyright 1942 by Budd Schulberg, renewed 1970 by Budd Schulberg. Reprinted by permission of Russell & Volkening as agents for the author.
"Dancing Dan's Christmas" by Damon Runyon. Copyright renewed 1959 by Mary Runyon McCann and Damon Runyon, Jr. as children of the author. Reprinted by permission of Sheldon Abend, President, American Play Company, Inc.
"Merry Christmas" from *Alarms and Diversions* by James Thurber, published by Harper & Row. Copyright © 1957 James Thurber. Copyright © 1985 Helen Thurber and Rosemary A. Thurber. Reprinted by permission.
"The Tree That Didn't Get Trimmed" from *Essays* by Christopher Morley, Copyright 1919, 1947 Christopher Morley. Reprinted by permission of the Estate of Christopher Morley.

LIBRARY OF CONGRESS CATALOGING IN PUBLICATION DATA

Christmas tales : celebrated authors on the magic on the season / with photographs by Steve Lovi
p. cm.
ISBN: 0-670-83810-1 1. Christmas stories, American. I. Lovi, Steve
PS648.C45C46 1992
813'.010833--dc20 92-54066

Printed in Japan

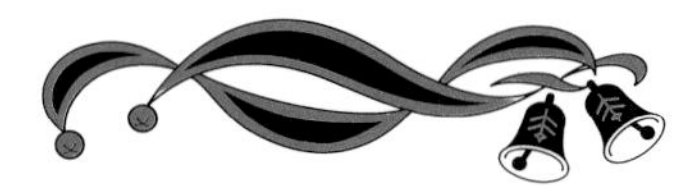

DEDICATION

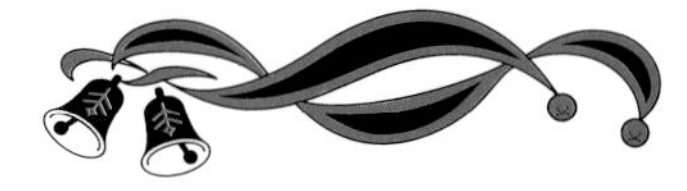

To
My Father
For His Art
Of Giving

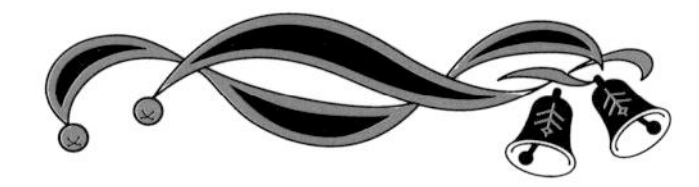

CONTENTS

Christmas Tales

CRISP NEW BILLS FOR MR. TEAGLE

Coming down in the elevator, Clement Teagle noticed an unwonted cordiality in Steve, the elevator boy, and Harry, the doorman, but thought nothing of it until he stopped at the bank on the corner to cash a check and noticed the date.

December the twenty-fourth.

"Good gosh," Mr. Teagle thought, "I haven't bought a present for Essie yet."

Then he remembered Steve and Harry.

His eye caught a legend on a Christmas placard on the wall. "It is more blessed to give than to receive," said the placard.

"Oh, yeah?" remarked Mr. Teagle, who, alas, was somewhat of a cynic.

Grumbling, he tore up the check he had started to write, and made out another, for a larger amount.

FRANK SULLIVAN

"Will you please give me new bills?" he asked.

"Indeed I shall," said Mr. Freyer, the teller, cordially.

He counted out one hundred dollars in new bills — crisp new bills — and passed them over to Mr. Teagle.

Then he tore up the check and handed the fragments to Mr. Teagle.

"Don't be alarmed, Mr. Teagle," said Mr. Freyer. "The bank of the Manhattan Company wants you to accept that one hundred dollars as a slight token of its esteem, with its best wishes for a merry Christmas. You have been a loyal depositor here these many years. You have overdrawn fewer times than most of your fellow-depositors. You never argue about your monthly statements. You never feel insulted when a new teller identifies your signature before cashing your check. You are the kind of depositor who makes banking a joy, and I want to take this opportunity to tell you that we fellows around here, although we are not very demonstrative about that sort of thing, love you very much. A merry Christmas to you."

"You mean the bank is *giving* me this money?" said Mr. Teagle.

"That is the impression I was trying to convey," said Mr. Freyer, with a chuckle.

"Why — uh, thanks, Mr. Freyer. And — and thank the bank. This is — um — quite a surprise."

"Say no more about it, Mr. Teagle. And every Christmas joy to you, sir."

When Mr. Teagle left the bank he was somewhat perturbed, and a little stunned. He went back to the apartment to place the crisp new bills in envelopes for the boys, and as he left the elevator at his floor, Steve handed him an envelope.

"Merry Christmas, Mr. Teagle," said Steve.

"Thanks, Steve," said Mr. Teagle. "I'll — I'll be wishing you one a little later," he said significantly.

"You don't need to, Mr. Teagle," said Steve. "A man like you wishes the whole world a merry Christmas every day, just by living."

"Oh, Steve, damn nice of you to say that, but I'm sure it's not deserved," said Mr. Teagle, modestly struggling with a feeling that Steve spoke no more than the simple truth.

"Well, I guess we won't argue about *that*," said Steve, gazing affectionately at Mr. Teagle.

"I really believe that lad meant it," thought Mr. Teagle, as he let himself into the apartment. "I really believe he did."

Mr. Teagle opened the envelope Steve had handed him. A crisp new five-dollar bill fell out.

Downstairs in the lobby, a few minutes later, Steve was protesting.

"I tell you it wasn't a mistake, Mr. Teagle. I put the bill in there on purpose. For *you*."

"Steve, I couldn't take — "

"But you *can* take it, and you *will*, Mr. Teagle. And a very merry Christmas to you."

"Then you accept this, Steve, and a merry Christmas to *you*."

"Oh, no, Mr. Teagle. Not this year. You have been pretty swell to we fellows all the years you've lived here. Now it's our turn."

"You bet it is," said Harry the doorman, joining them and pressing a crisp new ten-dollar bill into Mr. Teagle's hand. "Merry Christmas, Mr. Teagle. Buy yourself something foolish with this. I only wish it could be more, but I had rather a bad year in the market."

"I think the boys on the night shift have a little surprise for Mr. Teagle, too," said Steve, with a twinkle in his eye.

Just then the superintendent came up.

"Well, well, well," he said jovially. "Who have we got here? Mr. Teagle, it may interest you to hear that I've been having a little chat about you with a certain old gentleman with a long, snowy beard and twinkling little eyes. Know who I mean?"

"Santa Claus?" Mr. Teagle asked.

"None other. And guess what! He asked me if you had been a good boy this year, and I was delighted to be able to tell him you had been, that you hadn't complained about the heat, hadn't run your radio after eleven at night, and hadn't had any late parties. Well, sir, you should have seen old Santa's face. He was tickled to hear it. Said he always knew you were a good boy. And what do you suppose he did?"

"What?" asked Mr. Teagle.

"He asked me to give you this and to tell you to buy yourself something for Christmas with it. Something foolish."

The super pressed a crisp new twenty-dollar bill upon Mr. Teagle.

"Merry Christmas, Mr. Teagle," said the super.

"Merry Christmas, Mr. Teagle," said Steve the elevator boy.

"Merry Christmas, Mr. Teagle," said Harry the doorman.

"Merry Christmas," said Mr. Teagle, in a voice you could scarcely hear. Remembering that he had to buy a present for Essie, he walked out, with the air of a bewildered gazelle. He was in a very, very puzzled state of mind as he walked down East Fifty-first Street, an agitation which did not subside when the proprietor of a cigar store on Third Avenue rushed out, pressed a box of cigars on him, cried, "Merry Christmas, stranger!" and rushed back into his shop without another word.

To rush out of your store and give a box of cigars to a perfect stranger! And those boys at the apartment house! *And* the super!

Mr. Teagle thought of the many times he had grumbled at being kept waiting a few minutes for the elevator or for a taxi. He felt ashamed. "By George," Mr. Teagle thought, "maybe Dickens was right."

Mr. Teagle approached the business of choosing a present for his wife in a far less carping spirit than was his Christmas wont.

"I'll get Essie something that'll knock her eye out," he thought. "She's a good old girl and she deserves a lot of credit for living with a grouch like me all these years. The best is none too good for her."

Suiting the action to the word, Mr. Teagle turned in at Cartier's and asked to see some square-cut emeralds. He selected one that could have done duty on a traffic light.

"I'm afraid I haven't the cash on me," he told the clerk. "I'll give you a check, and you can call the bank and verify — "

"Thank will not be necessary, sir," said the clerk, with a radiant smile. "You are Mr. Clement Teagle, I believe. In that case, Cartier wishes you to accept this trinket with the Christmas greetings of the firm. We are only sorry that you did not see fit to choose a diamond stomacher. Cartier will feel honored that one of its emeralds is adorning the finger of the wife of a man like Clement Teagle, a man four-square, a man who is a credit — All right, all right, all *right*, Mr. Teagle! Not another word, please. Cartier is adamant. You take this emerald or we may grow ugly about it. And don't lose it, sir, or I venture to say your good wife will give you Hail Columbia. Good day, sir, and God rest ye."

Mr. Teagle found himself on the street. He accosted the first passerby.

"Excuse me, stranger, but would you mind pinching me?"

"Certainly not, certainly not," said the stranger, cheerily. "There. Feel better?"

"Yes. Thank you very much," said Mr. Teagle.

"Here, buy yourself something for Christmas," said the stranger, pressing Mr. Teagle's hand. Mr. Teagle looked in the hand and found himself the possessor of a crisp new fifty-dollar bill.

At Fifth Avenue and Fifty-seventh Street, a Park & Tilford attendant rushed out and draped a huge basket, bedecked with ribbons and holly, on Mr. Teagle's arm.

"Everything drinkable for the Yuletide dinner, with love and kisses from Park & Tilford," whispered the clerk jovially. "Tell your wife to be sure and put the champagne in ice early, so it will be nice and cold."

"Oh, come on, come on," protested the butcher at Madison Avenue and Sixty-first Street. "Don't tell me you're too loaded down to carry a simple little turkey home, with the affectionate Christmas wishes of Shaffer's Market."

Mr. Shaffer laughed the rich laugh of the contented butcher.

"Don't take me too seriously when I say simple little turkey," he said. "That bird you got would make Roosevelt's Christmas turkey look like a hummingbird. An undernourished hummingbird. Pay for it? Certainly you won't pay for it! What do you take me for? It's Christmas. And you are Clement Teagle."

"Am I?" said Mr. Teagle, humbly.

Long before he reached home, Mr. Teagle had had such a plethora of gifts pressed upon him by friendly strangers that there was nothing to do but load them into a taxicab. And Mr. Teagle was not quite as surprised as he might have been earlier in the day when the driver refused to accept any money, but grinned and said: "Let's just charge this trip to good old St. Nick."

"Why, Clem!" said Mrs. Teagle, when, with the aid of the entire house staff, Mr. Teagle had deposited his gifts in the dining room. "Why, Clem, I already *bought* a turkey! Clem, you've been drinking."

"I have *not*!" Mr. Teagle shouted.

"Well, don't get on your high horse," said Mrs. Teagle. "It's Christmas Eve. I don't mind. Only — you know your stomach. And you do look funny."

"I may look funny, but I have not been drinking," Mr. Teagle insisted. "Look! H-h-h-h-h-h."

His breath was as the new-mown hay.

"See what I got you for Christmas, Essie." Mrs. Teagle opened the jewel case and the emerald gleamed up at her. It was a moment before she could speak.

"No, Clem," she said. "You work too hard for your money. I don't deserve this. I won't take it from you. You've been too good to me as it is. I don't want any Christmas present from you, dear. I want to *give* you one — and oh, by the way, Clem, before I forget it, the funniest thing happened this afternoon. The income-tax man was here, the federal income-tax man. Said he just dropped in to wish you a merry Christmas. He left this check for your entire last year's income tax. He said the Government wants to give it back to you as a token of affection and in recognition of your many superb qualities as a citizen and — oh, I can't remember everything he said, but he made quite a flowery speech about you, dear — Why, Clem, what's the matter?"

Mr. Teagle had burst into tears.

"A merry Christmas, Essie," he said, through his sobs, and, in the language of Tiny Tim, "'God bless us every one.'"

The Burglar's Christmas

Two very shabby looking young men stood at the corner of Prairie Avenue and Eightieth Street, looking despondently at the carriages that whirled by. It was Christmas Eve, and the streets were full of vehicles; florists' wagons, grocers' carts and carriages. The streets were in that half-liquid, half-congealed condition peculiar to the streets of Chicago at that season of the year. The swift wheels that spun by sometimes threw the slush of mud and snow over the two young men who were talking on the corner.

"Well," remarked the elder of the two, "I guess we are at our rope's end, sure enough. How do you feel?"

"Pretty shaky. The wind's sharp to-night. If I had had anything to eat I mightn't mind it so much. There is simply no

WILLA CATHER

show. I'm sick of the whole business. Looks like there's nothing for it but the lake."

"O, nonsense, I thought you had more grit. Got anything left you can hock?"

"Nothing but my beard, and I am afraid they wouldn't find it worth a pawn ticket," said the younger man ruefully, rubbing the week's growth of stubble on his face.

"Got any folks anywhere? Now's your time to strike 'em if you have."

"Never mind if I have, they're out of the question."

"Well, you'll be out of it before many hours if you don't make a move of some sort. A man's got to eat. See here, I am going down to Longtin's saloon. I used to play the banjo in there with a couple of coons, and I'll bone him for some of his free-lunch stuff. You'd better come along, perhaps they'll fill an order for two."

"How far down is it?"

"Well, it's clear downtown, of course, 'way down on Michigan Avenue."

"Thanks, I guess I'll loaf around here. I don't feel equal to the walk, and the cars — well, the cars are crowded." His features drew themselves into what might have been a smile under happier circumstances.

"No, you never did like streetcars, you're too aristocratic. See here, Crawford, I don't like leaving you here. You ain't good company for yourself tonight."

"Crawford? O, yes, that's the last one. There have been so many I forget them."

"Have you got a real name, anyway?"

"O, yes, but it's one of the ones I've forgotten. Don't you worry about me. You go along and get your free lunch. I think I had a row in Longtin's place once. I'd better not show myself there again." As he spoke the young man nodded and turned slowly up the avenue.

He was miserable enough to want to be quite alone. Even the crowd that jostled by him annoyed him. He wanted to think about himself. He had avoided this final

reckoning with himself for a year now. He had laughed it off and drunk it off. But now, when all those artificial devices which are employed to turn our thoughts into other channels and shield us from ourselves had failed him, it must come. Hunger is a powerful incentive to introspection.

It is a tragic hour, that hour when we are finally driven to reckon with ourselves, when every avenue of mental distraction has been cut off and our own life and all its ineffaceable failures closes about us like the walls of that old torture chamber of the Inquisition. Tonight, as this man stood stranded in the streets of the city, his hour came. It was not the first time he had been hungry and desperate and alone. But always before there had been some outlook, some chance ahead, some pleasure yet untasted that seemed worth the effort, some face that he fancied was, or would be, dear. But it was not so tonight. The unyielding conviction was upon him that he had failed in everything, had outlived everything. It had been near him for a long time, that Pale Spectre. He had caught its shadow at the bottom of his glass many a time, at the head of his bed when he was sleepless at night, in the twilight shadows when some great sunset broke upon him. It had made life hateful to him when he awoke in the morning before now. But now it settled slowly over him, like night, the endless Northern nights that bid the sun a long farewell. It rose up before him like granite. From this brilliant city with its glad bustle of Yuletide he was shut off as completely as though he were a creature of another species. His days seemed numbered and done, sealed over like the little coral cells at the bottom of the sea. Involuntarily he drew that cold air through his lungs slowly, as though he were tasting it for the last time.

Yet he was but four and twenty, this man — he looked even younger — and he had a father someplace down east who had been very proud of him once. Well, he had taken his life into his own hands, and this was what he had made of it. That was all there was to be said. He could remember the hopeful things they used to say about him at college in the old days, before he had cut away and begun to live by his wits, and he found courage to smile at them now. They had read him wrongly. He knew now that he never had the essentials of success, only the superficial agility that is often mistaken for it. He was tow without the tinder, and he had burnt himself out at other people's fires. He had helped other people to make it win, but he himself — he had never touched an enterprise that had not failed eventually. Or, if it survived his connection with it, it left him behind.

His last venture had been with some ten-cent specialty company, a little lower than all the others, that had gone to pieces in Buffalo, and he had worked his way to Chicago by boat. When the boat made up its crew for the outward voyage, he was dispensed with as usual. He was used to that. The reason for it? O, there are so many reasons for failure! His was a very common one.

As he stood there in the wet under the streetlight he drew up his reckoning with the world and decided that it had treated him as well as he deserved. He had overdrawn his account once too often. There had been a day when he thought otherwise; when he had said he was unjustly handled, that his failure was merely the lack of proper adjustment between himself and other men, that someday he would be recognized and it would all come right. But he knew better than that now, and he was still man enough to bear no grudge against anyone — man or woman.

Tonight was his birthday, too. There seemed something particularly amusing in that. He turned up a limp coat collar to try to keep a little of the wet chill from his throat, and instinctively began to remember all the birthday parties he used to have. He was so cold and empty that his mind seemed unable to grapple with any serious question. He kept thinking about gingerbread and frosted cakes like a child. He could remember the splendid birthday parties his mother used to give him, when all the other little boys in the block came in their Sunday clothes and creaking shoes, with their ears still red from their mother's towel, and the pink and white birthday cake, and the stuffed olives and all the dishes of which he had been particularly fond, and how he would eat and eat and then go to bed and dream of Santa Claus. And in the morning he would awaken and eat again, until by night the family doctor arrived with his castor oil, and poor William used to dolefully say that it was altogether too much to have your birthday and Christmas all at once. He could remember, too, the royal birthday suppers he had given at college, and the stag dinners, and the toasts, and the music, and the good fellows who had wished him happiness and really meant what they said.

And since then there were other birthday suppers that he could not remember so clearly; the memory of them was heavy and flat, like cigarette smoke that has been shut in a room all night, like champagne that has been a day opened, a song that has been too often sung, an acute sensation that has been overstrained. They seemed tawdry and garish, discordant to him now. He rather wished he could forget them altogether.

Whichever way his mind now turned there was one thought that it could not escape, and that was the idea of food. He caught the scent of a cigar suddenly, and felt a sharp pain in the pit of his abdomen and a sudden moisture in his mouth. His cold hands clenched angrily, and for a moment he felt that bitter hatred of wealth, of ease, of everything that is well fed and well housed that is common to starving men. At any rate he had a right to eat! He had demanded great things from the world once: fame and wealth and admiration. Now it was simply bread — and he would have it! He looked about him quickly and felt the blood begin to stir in his veins. In all his straits he had never stolen anything, his tastes were above it. But tonight there would be no tomorrow. He was amused at the way in which the idea excited him. Was it possible there

was yet one more experience that would distract him, one thing that had power to excite his jaded interest? Good! He had failed at everything else, now he would see what his chances would be as a common thief. It would be amusing to watch the beautiful consistency of his destiny work itself out even in that role. It would be interesting to add another study to his gallery of futile attempts, and then label them all: "the failure as a journalist," "the failure as a lecturer," "the failure as a businessman," "the failure as a thief," and so on, like the titles under the pictures of the Dance of Death. It was time that Childe Roland came to the dark tower.

A girl hastened by him with her arms full of packages. She walked quickly and nervously, keeping well within the shadow, as if she were not accustomed to carrying bundles and did not care to meet any of her friends. As she crossed the muddy street, she made an effort to lift her skirt a little, and as she did so one of the packages slipped unnoticed from beneath her arm. He caught it up and overtook her. "Excuse me, but I think you dropped something."

She started, "O, yes, thank you, I would rather have lost anything than that."

The young man turned angrily upon himself. The package must have contained something of value. Why had he not kept it? Was this the sort of thief he would make? He ground his teeth together. There is nothing more maddening than to have morally consented to crime and then lack the nerve force to carry it out.

A carriage drove up to the house before which he stood. Several richly dressed women alighted and went in. It was a new house, and must have been built since he was in Chicago last. The front door was open and he could see down the hallway and up the staircase. The servant had left the door and gone with the guests. The first floor was brilliantly lighted, but the windows upstairs were dark. It looked very easy, just to slip upstairs to the darkened chambers where the jewels and trinkets of the fashionable occupants were kept.

Still burning with impatience against himself he entered quickly. Instinctively he removed his mud-stained hat as he passed quickly and quietly up the staircase. It struck him as being a rather superfluous courtesy in a burglar, but he had done it before he had thought. His way was clear enough, he met no one on the stairway or in the upper hall. The gas was lit in the upper hall. He passed the first chamber door through sheer cowardice. The second he entered quickly, thinking of something else lest his courage should fail him, and closed the door behind him. The light from the hall shone into the room through the transom. The apartment was furnished richly enough to justify his expectations. He went at once to the dressing case. A number of rings and small trinkets lay in a silver tray. These he put hastily in his pocket. He opened the upper drawer and found, as he expected, several leather cases. In the first he opened was a lady's watch, in the second a pair of old-fashioned bracelets; he seemed to dimly remember having seen bracelets like them before, somewhere. The third case was heavier, the spring was much worn, and it opened easily. It held a cup of some kind. He held it up to the light and then his strained nerves gave way and he uttered a sharp exclamation. It was the silver mug he used to drink from when he was a little boy.

The door opened, and a woman stood in the doorway facing him. She was a tall woman, with white hair, in evening dress. The light from the hall streamed in upon him, but she was not afraid. She stood looking at him a moment, then she threw out her hand and went quickly toward him.

"Willie, Willie! Is it you?"

He struggled to loose her arms from him, to keep her lips from his cheek. "Mother — you must not! You do not understand! O, my God, this is worst of all!" Hunger, weakness, cold, shame, all came back to him, and shook his self-control completely. Physically he was too weak to stand a shock like this. Why could it not have been an ordinary discovery, arrest, the station house and all the rest of it. Anything but this! A hard dry sob broke from him. Again he strove to disengage himself.

"Who is it says I shall not kiss my son? O, my boy, we have waited so long for this! You have been so long in coming, even I almost gave you up."

Her lips upon his cheek burnt him like fire. He put his hand to his throat, and spoke thickly and incoherently: "You do not understand. I did not know you were here. I came her to rob — it is the first time — I swear it — but I am a common thief. My pockets are full of your jewels now. Can't you hear me? I am a common thief!"

"Hush, my boy, those are ugly words. How could you rob your own house? How could you take what is your own? They are all yours, my son, as wholly yours as my great love — and you can't doubt that, Will, do you?"

That soft voice, the warmth and fragrance of her person stole through his chill, empty veins like a gentle stimulant. He felt as though all his strength were leaving him and even consciousness. He held fast to her and bowed his head on her strong shoulder, and groaned aloud.

"O, mother, life is hard, hard!"

She said nothing, but held him closer. And O, the strength of those white arms that held him! O, the assurance of safety in that warm bosom that rose and fell under his cheek! For a moment they stood so, silently. Then they heard a heavy step upon the stair. She led him to a chair and went out and closed the door. At the top of the staircase she met a tall, broad-shouldered man, with iron gray hair, and a face alert and stern. Her eyes were shining and her cheeks on fire, her whole face was one expression of intense determination.

"James, it is William in there, come home. You must keep him at any cost. If he goes this time, I go with him. O, James, be easy with him, he has suffered so." She broke from a command to an entreaty, and laid her hand on his shoulder. He looked questioningly at her a moment, then went in the room and quietly shut the door.

She stood leaning against the wall, clasping her temples with her hands and listening to the low indistinct sound of the voices within. Her own lips moved silently. She waited a long time, scarcely breathing. At last the door opened, and her husband came out. He stopped to say in a shaken voice,

"You go to him now, he will stay. I will go to my room. I will see him again in the morning."

She put her arm about his neck, "O, James, I thank you, I thank you! This is the night he came so long ago, you remember? I gave him to you then, and now you give him back to me!"

"Don't, Helen," he muttered. "He is my son, I have never forgotten that. I failed with him. I don't like to fail, it cuts my pride. Take him and make a man of him." He passed on down the hall.

She flew into the room where the young man sat with his head bowed upon his knee. She dropped upon her knees beside him. Ah, it was so good to him to feel those arms again!

"He is so glad, Willie, so glad! He may not show it, but he is as happy as I. He never was demonstrative with either of us, you know."

"O, my God, he was good enough," groaned the man. "I told him everything, and he was good enough. I don't see how either of you can look at me, speak to me, touch me." He shivered under her clasp again as when she had first touched him, and tried weakly to throw her off.

But she whispered softly,

"This is my right, my son."

Presently, when he was calmer, she rose. "Now, come with me into the library, and I will have your dinner brought there."

As they went downstairs she remarked apologetically, "I will not call Ellen tonight; she has a number of guests to attend to. She is a big girl now, you know, and came out last winter. Besides, I want you all to myself tonight."

When the dinner came, and it came very soon, he fell upon it savagely. As he ate she told him all that had transpired during the years of his absence, and how his father's business had brought them there. "I was glad when we came. I thought you would drift west. I seemed a good deal nearer to you here."

There was a gentle unobtrusive sadness in her tone that was too soft for a reproach.

"Have you everything you want? It is a comfort to see you eat."

He smiled grimly, "It is certainly a comfort to me. I have not indulged in this frivolous habit for some thirty-five hours."

She caught his hand and pressed it sharply, uttering a quick remonstrance.

"Don't say that! I know, but I can't hear you say it — it's too terrible! My boy, food had choked me many a time when I have thought of the possibility of that. Now take the old lounging chair by the fire, and if you are too tired to talk, we will just sit and rest together."

He sank into the depths of the big leather chair with the lions' heads on the arms, where he had sat so often in the days when his feet did not touch the floor and he was half afraid of the grim monsters cut in the polished wood. That chair seemed to speak to him of things long forgotten. It was like the touch of an old familiar friend. He felt a sudden yearning tenderness for the happy little boy who had sat there and dreamed of the big world so long ago. Alas, he had been dead many a summer, that little boy!

He sat looking up at the magnificent woman beside him. He had almost forgotten

how handsome she was; how lustrous and sad were the eyes that were set under that serene brow, how impetuous and wayward the mouth even now, how superb the white throat and shoulders! Ah, the wit and grace and fineness of this woman! He remembered how proud he had been of her as a boy when she came to see him at school. Then in the deep red coals of the grate he saw the faces of other women who had come since then into his vexed, disordered life. Laughing faces, with eyes artificially bright, eyes without depth or meaning, features without the stamp of high sensibilities. And he had left this face for such as those!

He sighed restlessly and laid his hand on hers. There seemed refuge and protection in the touch of her, as in the old days when he was afraid of the dark. He had been in the dark so long now, his confidence was so thoroughly shaken, and he was bitterly afraid of the night and of himself.

"Ah, mother, you make other things seem so false. You must feel that I owe you an explanation, but I can't make any, even to myself. Ah, but we make poor exchanges in life. I can't make out the riddle of it all. Yet there are things I ought to tell you before I accept your confidence like this."

"I'd rather you wouldn't, Will. Listen: Between you and me there can be no secrets. We are more alike than other people. Dear boy, I know all about it. I am a woman, and circumstances were different with me, but we are of one blood. I have lived all your life before you. You have never had an impulse that I have not known, you have never touched a brink that my feet have not trod. This is your birthday night. Twenty-four years ago I foresaw all this. I was a young woman then and I had hot battles of my own, and I felt your likeness to me. You were not like other babies. From the hour you were born you were restless and discontented, as I had been before you. You used to brace your strong little limbs against mine and try to throw me off as you did tonight.

Tonight you have come back to me, just as you always did after you ran away to swim in the river that was forbidden you, the river you loved because it was forbidden. You are tired and sleepy, just as you used to be then, only a little older and a little paler and a little more foolish. I never asked you where you had been then, nor will I now. You have come back to me, that's all in all to me. I know your every possibility and limitation, as a composer knows his instrument."

He found no answer that was worthy to give to talk like this. He had not found life easy since he had lived by his wits. He had come to know poverty at close quarters. He had known what it was to be gay with an empty pocket, to wear violets in his buttonhole when he had not breakfasted, and all the hateful shams of the poverty of idleness. He had been a reporter on a big metropolitan daily, where men grind out their brains on paper until they have not one idea left — and still grind on. He had worked in a real estate office, where ignorant men were swindled. He had sung in a comic opera chorus and played Harris in an *Uncle Tom's Cabin* company, and edited a socialist weekly. He had been dogged by debt and hunger and grinding poverty, until to sit here by a warm fire without concern as to how it would be paid for seemed unnatural.

He looked up at her questioningly. "I wonder if you know how much you pardon?"

"O, my poor boy, much or little, what does it matter? Have you wandered so far and paid such a bitter price for knowledge and not yet learned that love has nothing to do with pardon or forgiveness, that it only loves, and loves — and loves? They have not taught you well, the women of your world." She leaned over and kissed him, as no woman had kissed him since he left her.

He drew a long sigh of rich content. The old life, with all its bitterness and useless antagonism and flimsy sophistries, its brief delights that were always tinged with fear and distrust and unfaith, that whole miserable, futile, swindled world of Bohemia

seemed immeasurably distant and far away, like a dream that is over and done. And as the chimes rang joyfully outside and sleep pressed heavily upon his eyelids, he wondered dimly if the Author of this sad little riddle of ours were not able to solve it after all, and if the Potter would not finally mete out his all-comprehensive justice, such as none but he could have, to his Things of Clay, which are made in his own patterns, weak or strong, for his own ends; and if someday we will not awaken and find that all evil is a dream, a mental distortion that will pass when the dawn shall break.

My Christmas Carol

When I was a little boy, I lived with my parents in what was then a small suburb of Los Angeles called Hollywood. My father was general manager in charge of production for Firmament-Famous Artists-Lewin. It was a mouthful, but I used to have to remember the whole thing for the your-father-my-father arguments I was always having with a kid down the block whose old man was only an associate producer at Warner Brothers.

One of the things I remember most about Firmament-Famous Artists-Lewin was the way that studio and Christmas were all mixed up together in my mind. My earliest memory of the Christmas season is associated with a large studio truck, bearing the company's trademark, that always drove up to the house just before supper on Christmas

BUDD SCHULBERG

Eve. I would stand outside the kitchen door with my little sister and watch the driver and his helper carry into our house armload after armload of wonderful red and green packages — all for us. Sometimes the gleaming handlebars of a tricycle or the shiny wheels of a miniature fire engine would break through their bright wrappers, and I'd shout, "I know what that is!" until my mother would lead me away. Santa Claus still had so many houses to visit, she'd say, that I mustn't get in the way of these two helpers of his. Then I'd go down the street to argue the respective merits of our two studios with the Warner Brothers kid, or pass the time tormenting my little sister, perfectly content in the thought that the Firmament-Famous Artists-Lewin truck was the standard vehicle of transportation for Santa Claus in semitropical climates like Southern California.

On Christmas morning I had the unfortunate habit of rising at five o'clock, rushing across the hallway to my sister's room in annual disobedience of my mother's request to rise quietly, and shouting, "Merry Christmas, Sandra! Let's wake Mommy and Daddy and open our presents."

We ran down the hall into the master bedroom with its canopied twin beds. "Merry Christmas!" we shouted together. My father groaned, rolled over and pulled the covers further up over his head. He was suffering the after effects of the studio's annual all-day Christmas party from which he hadn't returned until after we had gone to sleep. I climbed up on the bed, crawling over him, and bounced up and down, chanting, "Merry Christmas, Merry Christmas . . ."

"Oh-h-h . . ." Father said, and flipped over on his belly. Mother shook his shoulder gently. "Sol, I hate to wake you, but the children won't go down without you."

Father sat up slowly, muttering something about its being still dark outside and demanding to know who had taken his bathrobe. Mother picked it up where he had

dropped it and brought it to him. It was black and white silk with an elegant embroidered monogram.

"The kids'll be opening presents for the next twelve hours," my father said. "It seems Goddamn silly to start opening them at five o'clock in the morning."

Downstairs there were enough toys, it seemed, to fill all the windows of a department store. The red car was a perfect model of a Pierce-Arrow, and probably only slightly less expensive, with a green leather seat wide enough for Sandra to sit beside me, and real headlights that turned on and off. There was a German electric train that passed through an elaborate Bavarian village in miniature. And a big scooter with rubber wheels and a gear shift just like our Cadillac's. And dozens more that I've forgotten. Sandra had a doll that was a life-size replica of Baby Peggy, which was Early Twenties for Margaret O'Brien, an imported silk Hungarian peasant costume from Lord & Taylor, a six-ounce bottle of French toilet water, and so many other things that we all had to help her unwrap them.

Just when we were reaching the end of this supply, people started arriving with more presents. That's the way it had been every Christmas since I could remember, men and women all dressed up dropping in all day long with packages containing wonderful things that they'd wait for us to unwrap. They'd sit around a while, laughing with my mother and father and lifting from James the butler's tray a cold yellow drink that I wasn't allowed to have, and then they'd pick us up and kiss us and tell us we were as pretty as my mother or as intelligent as my father and then there would be more laughing and hugging and hand-shaking and God bless you and then they'd be gone, and others would arrive to take their place. Sometimes there must have been ten or twenty all there at once and Sandra and I would be sort of sorry in a way because Mother and Father would be too busy with their guests to play with us. But it was nice to get all those presents.

I remember one tall dark man with a little pointed mustache who kissed Mother's hand when he came in. His present was wrapped in beautiful silvery paper and the blue ribbon around it felt thick and soft like one of Mother's evening dresses. Inside was a second layer of thin white tissue paper and inside of that was a handsome silver comb-and-brush set, just like my father's. Tied to it was a little card that I could read because it was printed and I could read almost anything then as long as it wasn't handwriting: "Merry Christmas to my future boss from Uncle Norman."

"Mommy," I said, "is Uncle Norman my uncle? You never told me I had an Uncle Norman. I have an Uncle Dave and an Uncle Joe and an Uncle Sam, but I never knew I had an Uncle Norman?"

I combed my hair with his silver comb suspiciously. "Did you give me this comb and brush . . . Uncle Norman."

I can still remember how white and even Norman's teeth looked when he smiled at me. "I'm a new uncle," he said. "Don't you remember the day your daddy brought you on my set and I signed your autograph book and I told you to call me Uncle Norman?"

Norman drank down the last of the foamy yellow stuff and carefully wiped off his mustaches with his pale-blue breast-pocket handkerchief. "Yes, I did, sonny," he said.

I turned on my mother accusingly. "But you said Santa Claus gives us all these presents."

This all took place, as I found out later, at a crucial moment in my relationship with S. Claus, when a child's faith was beginning to crumble under the pressure of suspicions. Mother was trying to keep Santa Claus alive for us as long as possible, I learned subsequently, so that Christmas would mean something more to us than a display of sycophancy on the part of Father's stars, directors, writers, and job-seekers.

"Norman signed his name to your comb and brush because he is one of Santa

Claus's helpers," Mother said. "Santa has so much work to do taking care of all the good little children in the world that he needs lots and lots of helpers."

My father offered one of his long, fat cigars to "Uncle" Norman and bit off the end of another one for himself.

"Daddy, is that true, what Mommy says?" I asked.

"You must always believe your mother, boy," my father said.

"I've got twenty-eleven presents already," Sandra said.

"You mean thirty-one," I said. "I've got thirty-two."

Sandra tore open a box that held an exquisite little gold ring, inlaid with amethyst, her birthstone.

"Let me read the card," I said. "'Merry Christmas, Sandra darling, from your biggest fan, Aunt Ruth.'"

Ruth was the pretty lady who played opposite Uncle Norman in one of my father's recent pictures. I hadn't been allowed to see it, but I used to boast to that Warner Brothers kid about how much better it was than anything Warners' could make.

Sandra, being very young, tossed Aunt Ruth's gold ring away and turned slowly in her hand the little box it had come in. "Look, it says numbers on it," she said. "Why are the numbers, Chris?"

I studied it carefully. "Ninety-five. That looks like dollars," I said. "Ninety-five dollars. Where does Santa Claus get all his money, Daddy?"

My father gave my mother a questioning look. "Er . . . what's that, son?" I had to repeat the question. "Oh . . . those aren't dollars, no . . . That's just the number Santa puts on his toys to keep them from getting all mixed up before he sends them down from the North Pole," my father said, and then he took a deep breath and another gulp of that yellow drink.

More people kept coming in all afternoon. More presents. More uncles and aunts. More Santa Claus's helpers. I never realized he had so many helpers. All afternoon the phone kept ringing, too. "Sol, you might as well answer it, it must be for you," my mother would say, and then I could hear my father laughing on the phone: "Thanks, L. B., and a merry Christmas to you . . . Thanks, Joe . . . Thanks, Mary . . . Thanks, Doug . . . Merry Christmas, Pola . . ." Gifts kept arriving late into the day, sometimes in big limousines and town cars, carried in by chauffeurs in snappy uniforms. No matter how my father explained it, it seemed to me that Santa must be as rich as Mr. Zukor.

Just before supper, one of the biggest stars in Father's pictures drove up in a Rolls-Royce roadster, the first one I had ever seen. She came in with a tall, broad-shouldered, sunburned man who laughed at anything anybody said. She was a very small lady and she wore her hair tight around her head like a boy's. She had on a tight yellow dress that only came down to the top of her knees. She and the man she was with had three presents for me and four for Sandra. She looked down at me and said, "Merry Christmas, you little darling," and before I could get away, she had picked me up and was kissing me. She smelled all funny, with perfumy sweetness mixed up with the way Father smelled when he came home from that Christmas party at the studio and leaned over my bed to kiss me when I was half asleep.

I didn't like people to kiss me, especially strangers. "Lemme go," I said.

"That's no way to act, sonny," the strange man said. "Why, right this minute every man in America would like to be in your shoes."

All the grownups laughed, but I kept squirming, trying to get away. "Aw, don't be that way, honey," the movie star said. "Why, I love men!"

They all laughed again. I didn't understand it so I started to cry. Then she put me down. "All right for you," she said, "if you don't want to be my boyfriend."

After she left, when I was unwrapping her presents, I asked my father, "Who is she? Is she one of Santa Claus's helpers, too?" Father winked at Mother, turned his head away, put his hand to his mouth and laughed into it, but I saw him. Mother looked at him the way she did when she caught me taking a piece of candy just before supper. "Her name is Clara, dear," she said. "She's one of Santa Claus's helpers, too."

And that's the way Christmas was, until one Christmas when a funny thing happened. The big Firmament-Famous Artists-Lewin truck never showed up. I kept looking for it all afternoon, but it never came. When it got dark and it was time for me to have my supper and go to bed and still no truck, I got pretty worried. My mind ran back through the year trying to remember some bad thing I might have done that Santa was going to punish me for. I had done lots of bad things, like slapping my sister and breaking my father's fountain pen, but they were no worse than the stuff I had pulled the year before. Yet what other reason could there possibly be for that truck not showing up?

Another thing that seemed funny about that Christmas Eve was that my father didn't bother to go to his studio Christmas party. He stayed home all morning and read aloud to me from a Christmas present he let me open a day early, a big blue book called *Typee*. And late that night when I tiptoed halfway down the stairs to watch my mother trim the tree that Santa was supposed to decorate, my father was helping her string the colored lights. Another thing different about that Christmas was that when Sandra and I ran in shouting and laughing at five, as we always did, my father got up just as soon as my mother.

When we went downstairs, we found almost as many presents as on other Christmas mornings. There was a nice fire engine from Uncle Norman, a cowboy suit from Aunt Ruth, a Meccano set from Uncle Adolph, something, in fact, from every one of Santa

Claus's helpers. No, it wasn't the presents that made this Christmas seem so different, it was how quiet everything was. Pierce-Arrows and Packards and Cadillacs didn't keep stopping by all day long with new presents for us. And none of the people like Norman and Ruth and Uncle Edgar, the famous director, and Aunt Betty, the rising ingenue, and Uncle Dick, the young star, and the scenario writer, Uncle Bill, none of them dropped in at all. James the butler was gone, too. For the first Christmas since I could remember, we had Father all to ourselves. Even the phone was quiet for a change. Except for a couple of real relatives, the only one who showed up at all was Clara. She came in around supper time with an old man whose hair was yellow at the temples and gray on top. Her face was very red and when she picked me up to kiss me, her breath reminded me of the Christmas before, only stronger. My father poured her and her friend the foamy yellow drink I wasn't allowed to have.

She held up her drink and said, "Merry Christmas, Sol. And may next Christmas be even merrier."

My father's voice sounded kind of funny, not laughing as he usually did. "Thanks, Clara," he said. "You're a pal."

"Nerts," Clara said. "Just because I don't wanna be a fair-weather friend like some of these other Hollywood bas — "

"Shhh, the children," my mother reminded her.

"Oh, hell, I'm sorry," Clara said. "But anyway, you know what I mean."

My mother looked from us to Clara and back to us again. "Chris, Sandra," she said. "Why don't you take your toys up to your own room and play? We'll be up later."

In three trips I carried up to my room all the important presents. I also took up a box full of cards that had been attached to the presents. As a bit of holiday homework, our penmanship teacher Miss Whitehead had suggested that we separate all Christmas-card

signatures into those of Spencerian grace and those of cramp-fingered illegibility. I played with my Meccano set for a while, I practiced twirling my lasso and I made believe Sandra was an Indian, captured her and tied her to the bedstead as my hero Art Acord did in the movies. I captured Sandra three or four times and then I didn't know what to do with myself, so I spread all the Christmas cards out on the floor and began sorting them just as Miss Whitehead had asked.

I sorted half a dozen, all quite definitely non-Spencerian, but it wasn't until I had sorted ten or twelve that I began to notice something funny. It was all the same handwriting. Then I came to a card of my father's. I was just beginning to learn how to read handwriting, and I wasn't very good at it yet, but I could recognize the three little bunched-together letters that spelled *Dad*. I held my father's card close to my eyes and compared it with the one from Uncle Norman. It was the same handwriting. Then I compared them with the one from Uncle Adolph. All the same handwriting. Then I picked up one of Sandra's cards, from Aunt Ruth, and held that one up against my father's. I couldn't understand it. My father seemed to have written them all.

I didn't say anything to Sandra about this, or to the nurse when she gave us our supper and put us to bed. But when my mother came in to kiss me good night I asked her why my father's handwriting was on all the cards. My mother turned on the light and sat on the edge of the bed.

"You don't really believe in Santa Claus anymore, do you?" she asked.

"No," I said. "Fred and Clyde told me all about it at school."

"Then I don't think it will hurt you to know the rest," my mother said. "Sooner or later you will have to know these things."

Then she told me what had happened. Between last Christmas and this one, my father had lost his job. He was trying to start his own company now. Lots of stars and directors had promised to go with him. But when the time had come to make good on their promises, they had backed out. Though I didn't fully understand it at the time, even in the simple way mother tried to explain it, I would say now that for most of those people the security of a major-company payroll had outweighed an adventure on Poverty Row — the name for the group of little studios where the independent producers struggled to survive.

So this had been a lean year for my father. We had sold one of the cars, let the butler go, and lived on a budget. As Christmas approached, Mother had cut our presents to a minimum.

"Anyway, the children will be taken care of," my father said. "The old gang will see to that."

The afternoon of Christmas Eve my father had had a business appointment, to see a banker about more financing for his program of pictures. When he came home, Sandra and I had just gone to bed, and Mother was arranging the presents around the tree. There weren't many presents to arrange, just the few they themselves had bought. There were no presents at all from my so-called aunts and uncles.

"My pals," Father said. "My admirers. My loyal employees."

Even though he had the intelligence to understand why those people had always sent us those expensive presents, his vanity, or perhaps I can call it his good nature, had led him to believe they did it because they genuinely were fond of Sandra and me.

"I'm afraid the kids will wonder what happened to all those Santa Claus's helpers," my mother said.

"Wait a minute," my father said. "I've got an idea. Those bastards are going to be Santa Claus's helpers whether they know it or not."

Then he rushed out to a toy store on Hollywood Boulevard and bought a gift for

every one of the aunts and uncles who were so conspicuously absent.

I remember, when my mother finished explaining, how I bawled. I don't know whether it was out of belated gratitude to my old man or whether I was feeling sorry for myself because all those famous people didn't like me as much as I thought they did. Maybe I was only crying because that first, wonderful and ridiculous part of childhood was over. From now on I would have to face a world in which there was not only no Santa Claus, but very, very few on-the-level Santa Claus's helpers.

Dancing Dan's Christmas

Now one time it comes on Christmas, and in fact it is the evening before Christmas, and I am in Good Time Charley Bernstein's little speakeasy in West Forty-seventh Street, wishing Charley a Merry Christmas and having a few hot Tom and Jerrys with him.

This hot Tom and Jerry is an old-time drink that is once used by one and all in this country to celebrate Christmas with, and in fact it is once so popular that many people think Christmas is invented only to furnish an excuse for hot Tom and Jerry, although of course this is by no means true.

But anybody will tell you that there is nothing that brings out the true holiday spirit like hot Tom and Jerry, and I hear that since Tom and Jerry goes out of style in the United States, the holiday

DAMON RUNYON

spirit is never quite the same.

The reason hot Tom and Jerry goes out of style is because it is necessary to use rum and one thing and another in making Tom and Jerry, and naturally when rum becomes illegal in this country Tom and Jerry is also against the law, because rum is something that is very hard to get around town these days.

For a while some people try making hot Tom and Jerry without putting rum in it, but somehow it never has the same old holiday spirit, so nearly everybody finally gives up in disgust, and this is not surprising, as making Tom and Jerry is by no means child's play. In fact, it takes quite an expert to make good Tom and Jerry, and in the days when it is not illegal a good hot Tom and Jerry maker commands good wages and many friends.

Now of course Good Time Charley and I are not using rum in the Tom and Jerry we are making, as we do not wish to do anything illegal. What we are using is rye whiskey that Good Time Charley gets on a doctor's prescription from a drugstore, as we are personally drinking this hot Tom and Jerry and naturally we are not foolish enough to use any of Good Time Charley's own rye in it.

The prescription for the rye whiskey comes from old Doc Moggs, who prescribes it for Good Time Charley's rheumatism in case Charley happens to get any rheumatism, as Doc Moggs says there is nothing better for rheumatism than rye whiskey, especially if it is made up in a hot Tom and Jerry. In fact, old Doc Moggs comes around and has a few seidels of hot Tom and Jerry with us for his own rheumatism.

He comes around during the afternoon, for Good Time Charley and I start making this Tom and Jerry early in the day, so as to be sure to have enough to last us over Christmas, and it is now along toward six o'clock, and our holiday spirit is practically one hundred percent.

Well, as Good Time Charley and I are expressing our holiday sentiments to each other over our hot Tom and Jerry, and I am trying to think up the poem about the night before Christmas and all through the house, which I know will interest Charley no little, all of a sudden there is a big knock at the front door, and when Charley opens the door who comes in carrying a large package under one arm but a guy by the name of Dancing Dan.

This Dancing Dan is a good-looking young guy, who always seems well-dressed, and he is called by the name of Dancing Dan because he is a great hand for dancing around and about with dolls in night clubs, and other spots where there is any dancing. In fact, Dan never seems to be doing anything else, although I hear rumors that when he is not dancing he is carrying on in the most illegal manner at one thing and another. But of course you can always hear rumors in this town about anybody, and personally I am rather fond of Dancing Dan as he always seems to be getting a great belt out of life.

Anybody in town will tell you that Dancing Dan is a guy with no Barnaby whatever in him, and in fact he has about as much gizzard as anybody around, although I wish to say I always question his judgment in dancing so much with Miss Muriel O'Neill, who works in the Half Moon night club. And the reason I question his judgment in this respect is because everybody knows that Miss Muriel O'Neill is a doll who is very well thought of by Heine Schmitz, and Heine Schmitz is not such a guy as will take kindly to anybody dancing more than once and a half with a doll that he thinks well of.

This Heine Schmitz is a very influential citizen of Harlem, where he has large interests in beer, and other business enterprises, and it is by no means violating any confidence to tell you that Heine Schmitz will just as soon blow your brains out as look at you. In fact, I hear sooner. Anyway, he is not a guy to monkey with and many citizens take the trouble to advise Dancing Dan that he is not only away out of line in dancing with Miss Muriel O'Neill, but that he is knocking his own price down to where he is no price at all.

But Dancing Dan only laughs ha-ha, and goes on dancing with Miss Muriel O'Neill any time he gets a chance, and Good Time Charley says he does not blame him, at that, as Miss Muriel O'Neill is so beautiful that he will be dancing with her himself no matter what, if he is five years younger and can get a Roscoe out as fast as in the days when he runs with Paddy the Link and other fast guys.

Well, anyway, as Dancing Dan comes in he weighs up the joint in one quick peek, and then he tosses the package he is carrying into a corner where it goes plunk, as if there is something very heavy in it, and then he steps up to the bar alongside of Charley and me and wishes to know what we are drinking.

Naturally we start boosting Hot Tom and Jerry to Dancing Dan, and he says he will take a crack at it with us, and after one crack, Dancing Dan says he will have another crack, and Merry Christmas to us with it, and the first thing anybody knows it is a couple of hours later and we are still having cracks at the hot Tom and Jerry with Dancing Dan, and Dan says he never drinks anything so soothing in his life. In fact, Dancing Dan says he will recommend Tom and Jerry to everyone he knows, only he doesn't know anybody good enough for Tom and Jerry, except maybe Miss Muriel O'Neill, and she does not drink anything with drugstore rye in it.

Well, several times while we are drinking this Tom and Jerry, customers come to the door of Good Time Charley's little speakeasy and knock, but by now Charley is commencing to be afraid they will wish Tom and Jerry, too, and he does not feel we will have enough for ourselves, so he hangs out a sign which says "Closed on Account of Christmas," and the only one he will let in is a guy by the name of Ooky, who is nothing but an old rum-dum, and who is going around all week dressed like Santa Claus and carrying a sign advertising Moe Lewinsky's clothing joint around in Sixth Avenue.

This Ooky is still wearing his Santa Claus outfit when Charley lets him in, and the reason Charley lets him in, and the reason Charley permits such a character as Ooky in his joint is because Ooky does the porter work for Charley when he is not Santa Claus for Moe Lewinsky, such as sweeping out, and washing the glasses, and one thing and another.

Well, it is about nine-thirty when Ooky comes in, and his puppies are aching, and he is still petered out generally from walking up and down and here and there in his sign, for any time a guy is Santa Claus for Moe Lewinsky he must earn his dough. In fact, Ooky is so fatigued, and his puppies hurt him so much that Dancing Dan and Good Time Charley and I all feel very sorry for him, and invite him to have a few mugs of hot Tom and Jerry with us, and wish him plenty of Merry Christmas.

But old Ooky is not accustomed to Tom and Jerry and after about the fifth mug he folds up in a chair, and goes right to sleep on us. He is wearing a pretty good Santa Claus make-up, what with a nice red suit trimmed with white cotton, and a wig, and false nose, and long white whiskers, and a big sack stuffed with excelsior on his back and if I do not know Santa Claus is not apt to be such a guy as will snore loud enough to rattle the windows, I will think Ooky is Santa Claus sure enough.

Well, we forget Ooky and let him sleep, and go on with our hot Tom and Jerry, and in the meantime we try to think up a few songs appropriate to Christmas, and Dancing Dan finally renders My Dad's Dinner Pail in a nice baritone and very loud, while I do first rate with Will You Love Me in December As You Do in May? But personally I will always think Good Time Charley Bernstein is a little out of line trying to sing a

hymn in Jewish on such an occasion, and it causes words between us.

While we are singing many customers come to the door and knock, and then they read Charley's sign, and this seems to cause some unrest among them, and some of them stand outside saying it is a great outrage, until Charley sticks his noggin out the door and threatens to bust somebody's beezer if they do not go on about their business and stop disturbing peaceful citizens.

Naturally the customers go away, as they do not wish to get their beezers busted, and Dancing Dan and Charley and I continue drinking our hot Tom and Jerry, and with each Tom and Jerry we are wishing one another a very Merry Christmas, and sometimes a very Happy New Year, although of course this does not go for Good Time Charley as yet, because Charley has his New Year separate from Dancing Dan and me.

By and by we take to waking Ooky up in his Santa Claus outfit and offering him more hot Tom and Jerry, and wishing him Merry Christmas, but Ooky only gets sore and calls us names, so we can see that he does not have the right holiday spirit in him, and let him alone until along about midnight when Dancing Dan wishes to see how he looks as Santa Claus.

So Good Time Charley and I help Dancing Dan pull off Ooky's outfit and put it on Dan, and this is easy as Ooky only has this Santa Claus outfit on over his ordinary clothes, and he does not even wake up when we are undressing him out of the Santa Claus uniform.

Well, I wish to say I see many a Santa Claus in my time, but I never see a better looking Santa Claus than Dancing Dan, especially after he gets the wig and white whiskers fixed just right, and we put a sofa pillow that Good Time Charley happens to have around the joint for the cat to sleep on down his pants and give Dancing Dan a nice fat stomach such as Santa Claus is bound to have.

In fact, after Dancing Dan looks at himself in a mirror awhile he is greatly pleased with his appearance, while Good Time Charley is practically hysterical, although personally I am beginning to resent Charley's interest in Santa Claus, and Christmas generally, as he by no means has any claim on these matters. But then I remember Charley furnishes the hot Tom and Jerry, so I am more tolerant toward him.

"Well," Charley finally says, "it is a great pity we do not know where there are some stockings hung up somewhere, because then," he says, "you can go around and stuff things in these stockings, as I always hear this is the main idea of a Santa Claus. But," Charley says, "I do not suppose anybody in this section has any stockings hung up, or if they have," he says, "the chances are they are so full of holes they will not hold anything. Anyway," Charley says, "even if there are any stockings hung up we do not have anything to stuff in them, although personally," he says, "I will gladly donate a few pints of Scotch."

Well, I am pointing out that we have no reindeer and that Santa Claus is bound to look like a terrible sap if he goes around without any reindeer, but Charley's remarks seem to give Dancing Dan an idea, for all of a sudden he speaks as follows:

"Why," Dancing Dan says, "I know where a stocking is hung up. It is hung up at Miss Muriel O'Neill's flat over here in West Forty-ninth Street. This stocking is hung up by nobody but a party by the name of Gammer O'Neill, who is Miss Muriel O'Neill's grandmamma," Dancing Dan says. "Gammer O'Neill is going on ninety-odd," he says, "and Miss Muriel O'Neill tells me she can not hold out much longer, what with one thing and another, including being a little childish in spots.

"Now," Dancing Dan says, "I remember Miss Muriel O'Neill is telling me just the other night how Gammer O'Neill hangs up her stockings on Christmas Eve all her life, and," he says, "I judge from what Miss Muriel O'Neill says that the old doll always believes Santa Claus will come along some Christmas and fill the stocking full of beautiful gifts. But," Dancing Dan says, "Miss Muriel O'Neill tells me Santa Claus never does this, although Miss Muriel O'Neill personally always takes a few gifts home and pops them into the stocking to make Gammer O'Neill feel better.

"But, of course," Dancing Dan says, "these gifts are nothing much because Miss Muriel O'Neill is very poor, and proud, and also good, and will not take a dime off anybody and I can lick the guy who says she will, although," Dancing Dan says, "between me, and Heine Schmitz, and a raft of other guys I can mention, Miss Muriel O'Neill can take plenty."

Well, I know that what Dancing Dan states about Miss Muriel O'Neill is quite true, and in fact it is a matter that is often discussed on Broadway, because Miss Muriel O'Neill cannot get more than twenty bobs per week working at the Half Moon, and it is well known to one and all that this no kind of dough for a doll as beautiful as Miss Muriel O'Neill.

"Now," Dancing Dan goes on, "it seems that while Gammer O'Neill is very happy to get whatever she finds in her stocking on Christmas morning, she does not understand why Santa Claus is not more liberal, and," he says, "Miss Muriel O'Neill is saying to me that she only wishes she can give Gammer O'Neill one real big Christmas before the old doll puts her checks back in the rack.

"So," Dancing Dan states, "here is a job for us. Miss Muriel O'Neill and her grandmamma live all alone in this flat over in West Forty-ninth Street, and," he says, "at such an hour as this Miss Muriel O'Neill is bound to be working, and the chances are Gammer O'Neill is sound asleep, and we will just hop over there and Santa Claus will fill up her stocking with beautiful gifts."

Well, I say, I do not see where we are going to get any beautiful gifts at this time of night, what with all the stores being closed, unless we dash into an all-night drugstore and buy a few bottles of perfume and a bum toilet set as guys always do when they forget about their ever-loving wives until after store hours on Christmas Eve, but Dancing Dan says never mind about this, but let us have a few more Tom and Jerrys first.

So we have a few more Tom and Jerrys, and then Dancing Dan picks up the package he heaves into the corner, and dumps most of the excelsior out of Ooky's Santa Claus sack, and puts the bundle in, and Good Time Charley turns out all the lights but one, and leaves a bottle of Scotch on the table in front of Ooky for a Christmas gift, and away we go.

Personally, I regret very much leaving the hot Tom and Jerry, but then I am also very enthusiastic about going along to help Dancing Dan play Santa Claus, while Good Time Charley is practically overjoyed, as it is the first time in his life Charley is ever mixed up in so much holiday spirit. In fact, nothing will do Charley but that we stop in a couple of spots and have a few drinks to Santa Claus' health, and these visits are a big success, although everybody is much surprised to see Charley and me with Santa Claus, especially Charley, although nobody recognizes Dancing Dan.

But of course there are no hot Tom and Jerrys in these spots we visit, and we have to drink whatever is on hand, and personally I will always believe that the noggin I have on me afterwards comes of mixing the drinks we get in these spots with my Tom and Jerry.

As we go up Broadway, headed for Forty-ninth Street, Charley and I see many citizens we know and give them a large hello, and wish them Merry Christmas, and some of these citizens shake hands with Santa Claus, not knowing he is nobody but Dancing Dan, although later I understand there is some gossip among these citizens because they claim a Santa Claus with such a breath on him as our Santa Claus has is a little out of line.

And once we are somewhat embarrassed when a lot of little kids going home with their parents from a late Christmas party somewhere gather about Santa Claus with shouts of childish glee, and some of them wish to climb up Santa Claus' legs. Naturally, Santa Claus gets a little peevish, and calls them a few names, and one of the parents comes up and wishes to know what is the idea of Santa Claus using such language, and Santa Claus takes a punch at the parent, all of which is no doubt most astonishing to the little kids who have an idea of Santa Claus as a very kindly old guy. But of course they do not know about Dancing Dan mixing the liquor we get in the spots we visit with his Tom and Jerry, or they will understand how even Santa Claus can lose his temper.

Well, finally we arrive in front of the place where Dancing Dan says Miss Muriel O'Neill and her grandmamma live, and it is nothing but a tenement house not far back of Madison Square Garden, and furthermore it is a walk-up, and at this time there are no lights burning in the joint except a gas jet in the main hall, and by the light of this jet we look at the names on the letter boxes, such as you always find in the hall of these joints, and we see that Miss Muriel O'Neill and her grandmamma live on the fifth floor.

This is the top floor, and personally I do not like the idea of walking up five flights of stairs, and I am willing to let Dancing Dan and Good Time Charley go, but Dancing Dan insists we must all go, and finally I agree because Charley is commencing to argue that the right way for us to do is to get on the roof and let Santa Claus go down a chimney, and is making so much noise I'm afraid he will wake somebody up.

So up the stairs we climb and finally we come to a door on the top floor that has a little card in the slot that says O'Neill, so we know we reach our destination. Dancing Dan first tries the knob, and right away the door opens, and we are in a little two- or three-room flat, with not much furniture in it, and what furniture there is is very poor. One single gas jet is burning near a bed in a room just off the one the door opens into, and by this light we see a very old doll is sleeping on the bed, so we judge this is nobody but Gammer O'Neill.

On her face is a large smile, as if she is dreaming of something very pleasant. On a chair at the head of the bed is hung a long black stocking, and it seems to be such a stocking as is often patched and mended, so I can see that what Miss Muriel O'Neill tells Dancing Dan about her grandmamma hanging up her stocking is really true, although up to this time I have my doubts.

Well, I am willing to pack in after one gander at the old doll, especially as Good Time Charley is commencing to prowl around the flat to see if there is a chimney where Santa Claus can come down, and is knocking things over, but Dancing Dan stands looking at Gammer O'Neill for a long time.

Finally he unslings the sack on his back, and takes out his package, and unties this package, and all of a sudden out pops a raft of big diamond bracelets, and diamond rings, and diamond brooches, and diamond necklaces, and I do not know what else in the way of diamonds, and Dancing Dan and I begin stuffing these diamonds into the stocking and Good Time Charley pitches in and helps us.

There are enough diamonds to fill the stocking to the muzzle, and it is no small stocking, at that, and I judge that Gammer O' Neill has a pretty fair set of bunting sticks when she is young. In fact, there are so many diamonds that we have enough left over to make a nice little pile on the chair after we fill the stocking plumb up, leaving a nice diamond-studded vanity case sticking out the top where we figure it

will hit Gammer O'Neill's eye when she wakes up.

And it is not until I get out in the fresh air again that all of a sudden I remember seeing large headlines in the afternoon papers about a five-hundred-G's stick-up in the afternoon of one of the biggest diamond merchants in Maiden Lane while he is sitting in his office, and I also recall once hearing rumors that Dancing Dan is one of the best lone-hand git-'em-guys in the world.

Naturally, I commence to wonder if I am in the proper company when I am with Dancing Dan, even if he is Santa Claus. So I leave him on the next corner arguing with Good Time Charley about whether they ought to go and find some more presents somewhere, and look for other stockings to stuff, and I hasten on home, and go to bed.

The next day I find I have such a noggin that I do not care to stir around, and in fact I do not stir around much for a couple of weeks.

Then one night I drop around to Good Time Charley's little speakeasy, and ask Charley what is doing.

"Well," Charley says, "many things are doing, and personally," he says, "I'm greatly surprised I do not see you at Gammer O'Neill's wake. You know Gammer O'Neill leaves this wicked old world a couple of days after Christmas," Good Time Charley says, "and," he says, "Miss Muriel O'Neill states that Doc Moggs claims that it is at least a day after she is entitled to go, but she is sustained," Charley says, "by great happiness in finding her stocking filled with beautiful gifts on Christmas morning.

"According to Miss Muriel O'Neill," Charley says, "Gammer O'Neill dies practically convinced that there is a Santa Claus, although of course," he says, "Miss Muriel O'Neill does not tell her the real owner of the gifts, an all-right guy by the name of Shapiro leaves the gifts with her after Miss Muriel O'Neill notifies him of the finding of same.

"It seems," Charley says, "this Shapiro is a tender-hearted guy, who is willing to keep Gammer O'Neill with us a little longer when Doc Moggs says leaving the gifts with her will do it.

"So," Charley says, "everything is quite all right, as the coppers cannot figure anything except that maybe the rascal who takes the gifts from Shapiro gets conscience stricken, and leaves them the first place he can, and Miss Muriel O'Neill receives a ten-G's reward for finding the gifts and returning them. And," Charley says, "I hear Dancing Dan is in San Francisco and is figuring on reforming and becoming a dancing teacher, so he can marry Miss Muriel O'Neill, and of course," he says, "we all hope and trust she never learns any details of Dancing Dan's career."

Well, it is Christmas Eve a year later that I run into a guy by the name of Shotgun Sam, who is mobbed up with Heine Schmitz in Harlem, and who is a very, very obnoxious character indeed.

"Well, well, well," Shotgun says, "the last time I see you is another Christmas Eve like this, and you are coming out of Good Time Charley's joint, and," he says, "you certainly have your pots on."

"Well, Shotgun," I say, "I am sorry you get such a wrong impression of me, but the truth is," I say, "on the occasion you speak of, I am suffering from a dizzy feeling in my head."

"It is all right with me," Shotgun says. "I have a tip this guy Dancing Dan is in Good Time Charley's the night I see you, and Mockie Morgan, and Gunner Jack and me are casing the joint, because," he says, "Heine Schmitz is all sored up at Dan over some doll, although of course," Shotgun says, "it is all right now, as Heine has another doll.

"Anyway," he says, "we never get to see Dancing Dan. We watch the joint from six-thirty in the evening until daylight Christmas morning, and nobody goes in all night but old Ooky the Santa Claus guy in his Santa Claus make-up, and," Shotgun says, "nobody comes out except you and Good Time Charley and Ooky.

"Well," Shotgun says, "it is a great break for Dancing Dan he never goes in or comes out of Good Time Charley's, at that, because," he says, "we are waiting for him on the second-floor front of the building across the way with some nice little sawed-offs, and are under orders from Heine not to miss."

"Well, Shotgun," I say, "Merry Christmas."

"Well, all right," Shotgun says, "Merry Christmas."

The Gift of the Magi

One dollar and eighty-seven cents. That was all. And sixty cents of it was in pennies. Pennies saved one and two at a time by bulldozing the grocer and the vegetable man and the butcher until one's cheeks burned with the silent imputation of parsimony that such close dealing implied. Three times Della counted it. One dollar and eighty-seven cents. And the next day would be Christmas.

There was clearly nothing to do but flop down on the shabby little couch and howl. So Della did it. Which instigates the moral reflection that life is made up of sobs, sniffles, and smiles, with sniffles predominating.

While the mistress of the home is gradually subsiding from the first stage to the second, take a look at the home. A furnished flat at eight dollars per week. It did

O. HENRY

not exactly beggar description, but it certainly had that word on the lookout for the mendicancy squad.

In the vestibule below was a letter box into which no letter would go, and an electric button from which no mortal finger could coax a ring. Also appertaining thereunto was a card bearing the name "Mr. James Dillingham Young."

The "Dillingham" had been flung to the breeze during a former period of prosperity when its possessor was being paid thirty dollars per week. Now, when the income was shrunk to twenty dollars, the letters of "Dillingham" looked blurred, as though they were thinking seriously of contracting to a modest and unassuming D. But whenever Mr. James Dillingham Young came home and reached his flat above he was called "Jim" and greatly hugged by Mrs. James Dillingham Young, already introduced to you as Della. Which is all very good.

Della finished her cry and attended to her cheeks with a powder puff. She stood by the window and looked out dully at a gray cat walking a gray fence in a gray backyard. Tomorrow would be Christmas Day, and she had only $1.87 with which to buy Jim a present. She had been saving every penny she could for months, with this result. Twenty dollars a week doesn't go far. Expenses had been greater than she had calculated. They always are. Only $1.87 to buy a present for Jim. Her Jim. Many a happy hour she had spent planning for something nice for him. Something fine and rare and sterling — something just a little bit near to being worthy of the honor of being owned by Jim.

There was a pier glass between the windows of the room. Perhaps you have seen a pier glass in an eight-dollar flat. A very thin and very agile person may, by observing his reflection in a rapid sequence of longitudinal strips, obtain a fairly accurate conception of his looks. Della, being slender, had mastered the art.

Suddenly she whirled from the window and stood before the glass. Her eyes were

shining brilliantly, but her face had lost its color within twenty seconds. Rapidly she pulled down her hair and let it fall to its full length.

Now, there were two possessions of the James Dillingham Youngs in which they both took a mighty pride. One was Jim's gold watch that had been his father's and his grandfather's. The other was Della's hair. Had the Queen of Sheba lived in the flat across the air shaft, Della would have let her hair hang out the window some day to dry just to depreciate Her Majesty's jewels and gifts. Had King Solomon been the janitor, with all his treasures piled up in the basement, Jim would have pulled out his watch every time he passed, just to see him pluck at his beard from envy.

So now Della's beautiful hair fell about her, rippling and shining like a cascade of brown waters. She did it up again nervously and quickly. Once she faltered for a minute and stood still while a tear or two splashed on the worn red carpet.

On went her old brown jacket; on went her old brown hat. With a whirl of skirts and with the brilliant sparkle still in her eyes, she fluttered out the door and down the stairs to the street.

Where she stopped the sign read: "Mme. Sofronie. Hair Goods of All Kinds." One flight up Della ran, and collected herself, panting. Madame, large, too white, chilly, hardly looked the "Sofronie."

"Will you buy my hair?" asked Della.

"I buy hair," said Madame. "Take yer hat off and let's have a sight at the looks of it."

Down rippled the brown cascade.

"Twenty dollars," said Madame, lifting the mass with a practiced hand.

"Give it to me quick," said Della.

Oh, and the next two hours tripped by on rosy wings. Forget the hashed metaphor. She was ransacking the stores for Jim's present.

She found it at last. It surely had been made for Jim and no one else. There was no other like it in any of the stores, and she had turned all of them inside out. It was a platinum watch chain, simple and chaste in design, properly proclaiming its value by substance alone and not by meretricious ornamentation — as all good things should do. It was even worthy of The Watch. As soon as she saw it she knew that it must be Jim's. It was like him. Quietness and value — the description applied to both. Twenty-one dollars they took from her for it, and she hurried home with the eighty-seven cents. With that chain on his watch Jim might be properly anxious about the time in any company. Grand as the watch was, he sometimes looked at it on the sly on account of the old leather strap that he used in place of a chain.

When Della reached home her intoxication gave way a little to prudence and reason. She got out her curling irons and lighted the gas and went to work repairing the ravages made by generosity added to love. Which is always a tremendous task, dear friends — a mammoth task.

Within forty minutes her head was covered with tiny close-lying curls that made her look wonderfully like a truant schoolboy. She looked at her reflection in the mirror long, carefully, and critically.

"If Jim doesn't kill me," she said to herself, "before he takes a second look at me, he'll say I look like a Coney Island chorus girl. But what could I do — oh! what could I do with a dollar and eighty-seven cents?"

At seven o'clock the coffee was made and the frying pan was on the back of the stove, hot and ready to cook the chops.

Jim was never late. Della doubled the watch chain in her hand and sat on the corner of the table near the door that he always entered. Then she heard his step on the stair away down on the first flight, and she turned white for just a moment. She had a habit of saying little silent prayers about the simplest everyday things, and now she whispered: "Please, God, make him think I am still pretty."

The door opened and Jim stepped in and closed it. He looked thin and very serious. Poor fellow, he was only twenty-two — and to be burdened with a family! He needed a new overcoat and he was without gloves.

Jim stepped inside the door, as immovable as a setter at the scent of quail. His eyes were fixed upon Della, and there was an expression in them that she could not read, and it terrified her. It was not anger, nor surprise, nor disapproval, nor horror, nor any of the sentiments that she had been prepared for. He simply stared at her fixedly with that peculiar expression on his face.

Della wriggled off the table and went for him.

"Jim, darling," she cried, "don't look at me that way. I had my hair cut off and sold it because I couldn't have lived through Christmas without giving you a present. It'll grow again — you won't mind, will you? I just had to do it. My hair grows awfully fast. Say 'Merry Christmas!' Jim, and let's be happy. You don't know what a nice — what a beautiful, nice gift I've got for you."

"You've cut off your hair?" asked Jim, laboriously, as if he had not arrived at that patent fact yet even after the hardest mental labor.

"Cut it off and sold it," said Della. "Don't you like me just as well, anyhow? I'm me without my hair, ain't I?"

Jim looked about the room curiously.

"You say your hair is gone?" he said, with an air almost of idiocy.

"You needn't look for it," said Della. "It's sold, I tell you — sold and gone, too. It's Christmas Eve, boy. Be good to me, for it went for you. Maybe the hairs on my head were numbered," she went on with a sudden serious sweetness, "but nobody could ever count my love for you. Shall I put the chops on, Jim?"

Out of his trance Jim seemed to quickly wake. He enfolded his Della. For ten seconds let us regard with discreet scrutiny some inconsequential object in the other direction. Eight dollars a week or a million a year — what is the difference? A mathematician or a wit would give you the wrong answer. The Magi brought valuable gifts, but that was not among them. This dark assertion will be illuminated later on.

Jim drew a package from his overcoat pocket and threw it upon the table.

"Don't make any mistake, Dell," he said, "about me. I don't think there's anything in the way of a haircut or a shave or shampoo that could make me like my girl any less. But if you'll unwrap that package you may see why you had me going awhile at first."

White fingers and nimble tore at the string and paper. And then an ecstatic scream of joy; and then, alas! a quick feminine change to hysterical tears and wails, necessitating the immediate employment of all the comforting powers of the lord of the flat.

For there lay The Combs — the set of combs that Della had worshiped for long in a Broadway window. Beautiful combs, pure tortoise shell, with jeweled rims — just the shade to wear in the beautiful vanished hair. They were expensive combs, she knew, and her heart had simply craved and yearned over them without the least hope of possession. And now they were hers, but the tresses that should have adorned the coveted adornments were gone.

But she hugged them to her bosom, and at length she was able to look up with dim eyes and a smile and say: "My hair grows so fast, Jim!"

And then Della leaped up like a little singed cat and cried, "Oh, oh!"

Jim had not yet seen his beautiful present. She held it out to him eagerly upon her open palm. The dull precious metal seemed to flash with a reflection of her bright and ardent spirit.

"Isn't it a dandy, Jim? I hunted all over town to find it. You'll have to look at the time a hundred times a day now. Give me your watch. I want to see how it looks on it."

Instead of obeying, Jim tumbled down on the couch and put his hands under the back of his head and smiled.

"Dell," he said, "let's put our Christmas presents away and keep 'em awhile. They're too nice to use just at present. I sold the watch to get the money to buy your combs. And now suppose you put the chops on."

The Magi, as you know, were wise men — wonderfully wise men — who brought gifts to the Babe in the manger. They invented the art of giving Christmas presents. Being wise, their gifts were no doubt wise ones, possibly bearing the privilege of exchange in case of duplication. And here I have lamely related to you the uneventful chronicle of two foolish children in a flat who most unwisely sacrificed for each other the greatest treasures of their house. But in a last word to the wise of these days let it be said that of all who give gifts these two were the wisest. Of all who give and receive gifts, such as they are wisest. Everywhere they are wisest. They are the Magi.

MERRY CHRISTMAS

It didn't surprise me to learn that Americans send out a billion and a half Christmas cards every year. That would have been my guess, give or take a quarter of a billion. Missing by 250 million is coming close nowayears, for what used to be called astronomical figures have now become the figures of earth. I am no longer staggered by the massive, but I can still be shaken by the minor human factors involved in magnificent statistics. A national budget of 71 thousand million is comprehensible to students of our warlike species, but who is to account for the rising sales of vodka in this nation — from 108,000 bottles in 1946 to 32,500,000 bottles in 1956? The complexities of federal debt and personal drinking are beyond my grasp, but I think I understand the Christmas card situation, or crisis.

JAMES THURBER

It disturbed me to estimate that two-fifths of the 1956 Christmas cards, or six hundred million, were received by people the senders barely knew and could count only as the most casual of acquaintances, and that approximately thirty million recipients were persons the senders had met only once, in a bar, on a West Indies cruise, at a doctor's office, or while fighting a grass fire in Westchester. The people I get Christmas cards from every year include a Jugoslav violist I met on the *Leviathan* in 1925, the doorman of a restaurant in Soho, a West Virginia taxi driver who is writing the biography of General Beauregard, the young woman who cured my hiccoughs at Dave Chasen's in 1939 (she twisted the little finger of my left hand and made me say Garbo backward), innumerable people who know what to do about my eye and were kind enough to tell me so in hotel lobbies and between the acts of plays, seven dog owners who told me at Tim's or Bleeck's that they have a dog exactly like the one I draw, and a lovely stranger in one of these saloons who snarled at a proud dog owner: "The only dog that looks like the dog this guy draws is the dog this guy draws."

The fifteen hundred million annual Yuletide greetings are the stamp and sign of the American character. We are a genial race, as neighborly abroad as at home, fond of perpetuating the chance encounter, the golden hour, the unique experience, the prewar vacation. "I think this calls for a drink" has long been one of our national slogans. Strangers take turns ordering rounds because of a shared admiration or disdain, a suddenly discovered mutual friend in Syracuse, the same college fraternity, a similar addiction to barracuda fishing. A great and lasting friendship rarely results, but the wife of each man adds the other's name to her Christmas list. The American woman who has been married ten years or longer, at least the ones I know, sends out about two hundred Christmas cards a year, many of them to persons on the almost forgotten fringe of friendship.

I had the good luck to be present one December afternoon in the living room of a

couple I know just as the mail arrived. The wife asked if we minded her glancing at the cards, but she had already read one. "My God!" she exclaimed. "The Spragues are still together! They were this really charming couple we met in Jamaica eight years ago. He had been a flier, I think, and had got banged up, and then he met Marcia — I think her name was Marcia." She glanced at the card again and said, "Yes, Marcia. Well, Philip was on leave in Bermuda and he saw her riding by in a carriage and simply knew she was the girl, although he had never laid eyes on her before in his life, so he ran out into the street and jumped up on the carriage step, and said, 'I'm going to marry you!" Would you believe it, he didn't even tell her his name, and of course he didn't know her from Adam — or Eve, I guess I ought to say — and they were married. They fell in love and got married in Bermuda. Her family was terribly opposed to it, of course, and so was his when they found out about hers, but they went right ahead anyway. It was the most romantic thing I ever heard of in my life. This was four or five years before we met them, and — "

"Why are you so astonished that they are still together?" I asked.

"Because their meeting was a kind of third-act curtain," said my friend's husband. "Boy meets girl, boy gets girl — as simple as that. All that's left is boy loses girl. Who the hell are Bert and Mandy?" he asked, studying a Christmas card.

Another greeting card category consists of those persons who send out photographs of their families every year. In the same mail that brought the greetings from Marcia and Philip, my friend found such a conversation piece. "My God, Lida is enormous!" she exclaimed. I don't know why women want to record each year, for two or three hundred people to see, the ravages wrought upon them, their mates, and their progeny by the artillery of time, but between five and seven percent of Christmas cards, at a rough estimate, are family groups, and even the most charitable recipient studies them for little signs of dissolution or derangement. Nothing cheers a woman more, I am afraid, than the proof that another woman is letting herself go, or has lost control of her figure, or is clearly driving her husband crazy, or is obviously drinking more than is good for her, or still doesn't know what to wear. Middle-aged husbands in such photographs are often described as looking "young enough to be her son," but they don't always escape so easily, and a couple opening envelopes in the season of mercy and goodwill sometimes handle a male friend or acquaintance rather sharply. "Good Lord!" the wife will say. "Frank looks like a sex-crazed shotgun slayer, doesn't he?" "Not to me," the husband may reply. "To me he looks more like a Wilkes-Barre dentist who is being sought by the police in connection with the disappearance of a choir singer."

Anyone who undertakes a comparative analysis of a billion and a half Christmas cards is certain to lose his way once in a while, and I now find myself up against more categories than I can handle. Somewhere in that vast tonnage of cardboard, for example, are — I am just guessing now — three hundred million cards from firms, companies, corporations, corner stores, and other tradespeople. In the old days they sent out calendars for the New Year, and skipped Christmas, but I figure they are now responsible for about a fifth of the deluge. Still another category includes inns, bars, restaurants, institutions, councils, committees, leagues, and other organizations. One of my own 1956 cards came from the Art Department of Immaculate Heart College, in Los Angeles, whose point of contact with me has eluded my memory. A certain detective agency used to send me a laconic word every December, but last year, for some disturbing reason, I was struck off the agency's list. I don't know how I got on it in the first place, since I have never employed a private investigator to shadow anybody, but it may be that I was one of the shadowed. The agency's slogan is "When we follow him he stays followed," and its card was invariably addressed to "Mr. James Ferber."

This hint of alias added a creepy note to the holidays, and, curiously enough, the sudden silence has had the same effect. A man who is disturbed when he hears from a detective agency, and when he doesn't, may be put down, I suppose, as a natural phenomenon of our nervous era.

I suddenly began wondering, in one of my onsets of panic, what becomes of all these cards. The lady in my house who adds two hundred items to the annual avalanche all by herself calmed my anxiety by telling me that most of them get burned. Later, I found out, to my dismay, that this is not actually true. There are at least nine million little girls who consider Christmas cards too beautiful to burn, and carefully preserve them. One mother told me that her garage contains fifteen large cartons filled with old Christmas cards. This, I am glad to say, is no problem of mine, but there is a major general somewhere who may have to deal with it one of these years if the accumulation becomes a national menace, hampering the movement of troops.

Ninety percent of women employ the annual greeting as a means of fending off a more frequent correspondence. One woman admitted to me that she holds at least a dozen friends at arm's, or year's, length by turning greeting cards into a kind of annual letter. The most a man will consent to write on a Christmas card is "Hi, boy!" or "Keep pitching," but a wife often manages several hundred words. These words, in most instances, have a way of dwindling with the march of the decades, until they become highly concentrated and even cryptic, such as "Will you ever forget that ox bice cake?" or "George says to tell Jim to look out for the 36." Thus the terrible flux of December mail is made up, in considerable part, of the forgotten and the meaningless. The money spent on all these useless cryptograms would benefit some worthy cause by at least three million dollars.

The sex behind most of the billion and a half Christmas cards is, of course, the

female. I should judge that about 75,000,000 cards are received annually by women from former cooks, secretaries, and hairdressers, the formerness of some of them going back as far as 1924. It is not always easy for even the most experienced woman card sender to tell an ex-hairdresser from someone she met on a night of high wind and Bacardi at Cambridge Beaches in Bermuda. The late John McNulty once solved this for my own wife by saying, "All hairdressers are named Delores." The wonderful McNulty's gift of inspired oversimplification, like his many other gifts, is sorely missed by hundreds of us. McNulty and I, both anti-card men, never exchanged Christmas greetings, except in person or on the phone. There was a time when I drew my own Christmas cards, but I gave it up for good after 1937. In that year I had drawn what purported to be a little girl all agape and enchanted in front of a strangely ornamented Christmas tree. The cards were printed in Paris and mailed to me, two hundred of them, in Italy. We were spending Christmas in Naples. The cards were held up at the border by the Italian authorities, agents of Mussolini who suspected everything, and returned to Paris. "I should think," commented an English friend of mine, "that two hundred copies of any drawings of yours might well give the authorities pause."

One couple, to conclude this survey on an eerie note, had sent out the same engraved Christmas card every year. Last time "From John and Joan" had undergone a little change. Joan had crossed out "John and." Her friends wonder just how many of these cheery greetings the predeceased Joan has left. So passed one husband, with only a pencil stroke to mark his going. Peace on earth, good will to women.

THE TREE THAT DIDN'T GET TRIMMED

If you walk through a grove of balsam trees you will notice that the young trees are silent; they are listening. But the old tall ones — especially the firs — are whispering. They are telling the story of The Tree That Didn't Get Trimmed. It sounds like a painful story, and the murmur of the old trees as they tell it is rather solemn; but it is an encouraging story for young saplings to hear. On warm autumn days when your trunk is tickled by ants and insects climbing, and the resin is hot and gummy in your knots, and the whole glade smells sweet, drowsy, and sad, and the hardwood trees are boasting of the gay colors they are beginning to show, many a young evergreen has been cheered by it.

All young fir trees, as you know by that story of Hans Andersen's — if you've

CHRISTOPHER MORLEY

forgotten it, why not read it again? — dream of being a Christmas Tree some day. They dream about it as young girls dream of being a bride, or young poets of having a volume of verse published. With the vision of that brightness and gaiety before them they patiently endure the sharp sting of the ax, the long hours pressed together on a freight car. But every December there are more trees cut down than are needed for Christmas. And that is the story that no one — not even Hans Andersen — has thought to put down.

The tree in this story should never have been cut. He wouldn't have been, but it was getting dark in the Vermont woods, and the man with the ax said to himself, "Just one more." Cutting young trees with a sharp, beautifully balanced ax is fascinating; you go on and on; there's a sort of cruel pleasure in it. The blade goes through the soft wood with one whistling stroke and the boughs sink down with a soft swish.

He was a fine, well-grown youngster, but too tall for his age; his branches were rather scraggly. If he'd been left there he would have been an unusually big tree some day; but now he was in the awkward age and didn't have the tapering shape and the thick, even foliage that people like on Christmas trees. Worse still, instead of running up to a straight, clean spire, his top was a bit lopsided, with a fork in it.

But he didn't know this as he stood with many others, leaning against the side wall of the greengrocer's shop. In those cold December days he was very happy, thinking of the pleasures to come. He had heard of the delights of Christmas Eve: the stealthy setting up of the tree, the tinsel balls and colored toys and stars, the peppermint canes and birds with spun-glass tails. Even that old anxiety of Christmas trees — burning candles — did not worry him, for he had been told that nowadays people use strings of tiny electric bulbs which cannot set one on fire. So he looked forward to the festival with a confident heart.

"I shall be very grand," he said. "I hope there will be children to admire me. It must

be a great moment when the children hang their stockings on you!" He even felt sorry for the first trees that were chosen and taken away. It would be best, he considered, not to be bought until Christmas Eve. Then, in the shining darkness someone would pick him out, put him carefully along the running board of a car, and away they would go. The tire chains would clack and jingle merrily on the snowy road. He imagined a big house with fire glowing on a hearth; the hushed rustle of wrapping paper and parcels being unpacked. Someone would say, "Oh, what a beautiful tree!" How erect and stiff he would brace himself in his iron tripod stand.

But day after day went by, one by one the other trees were taken, and he began to grow troubled. For everyone who looked at him seemed to have an unkind word. "Too tall," said one lady. "No, this one wouldn't do, the branches are too skimpy," said another. "If I chop off the top," said the greengrocer, "it wouldn't be so bad?" The tree shuddered, but the customer had already passed on to look at others. Some of his branches ached where the grocer had bent them upward to make his shape more attractive.

Across the street was a ten-cent store. Its bright windows were full of scarlet odds and ends; when the doors opened he could see people crowded along the aisles, cheerfully jostling one another with bumpy packages. A buzz of talk, a shuffle of feet, a constant ringing of cash drawers came noisily out of that doorway. He could see flashes of marvelous color, ornaments for luckier trees. Every evening, as the time drew nearer, the pavements were more thronged. The handsomer trees, not so tall as he but more bushy and shapely, were ranked in front of him; as they were taken away he could see the gaiety only too well. Then he was shown to a lady who wanted a tree very cheap. "You can have this one for a dollar," said the grocer. This was only one-third of what the grocer had asked for him at first, but even so the lady refused him and went across the street to buy a little artificial tree at the toy store. The man pushed him back carelessly, and he toppled over and fell alongside the wall. No one bothered to pick him up. He was almost glad, for now his pride would be spared.

Now it was Christmas Eve. It was a foggy evening with a drizzling rain; the alley alongside the store was thick with trampled slush. As he lay there among broken boxes and fallen scraps of holly strange thoughts came to him. In the still northern forest already his wounded stump was buried in forgetful snow. He remembered the wintry sparkle of the woods, the big trees with crusts and clumps of silver on their broad boughs, the keen singing of the lonely wind. He remembered the strong, warm feeling of his roots reaching down into the safe earth. That is a good feeling; it means to a tree just what it means to you to stretch your toes down toward the bottom of a well-tucked bed. And he had given up all this to lie here, disdained and forgotten, in a littered alley. The splash of feet, the chime of bells, the cry of cars went past him. He trembled a little with self-pity and vexation. "No toys and stockings for me," he thought sadly, and shed some of his needles.

Late that night, after all the shopping was over, the grocer came out to clear away what was left. The boxes, the broken wreaths, the empty barrels, and our tree with one or two others that hadn't been sold, all were thrown through the side door into the cellar. The door was locked and he lay there in the dark. One of his branches, doubled under him in the fall, ached so he thought it must be broken. "So this is Christmas," he said to himself.

All that day it was very still in the cellar. There was an occasional creak as one of the bruised trees tried to stretch itself. Feet went along the pavement overhead, and there was a booming of church bells, but everything had a slow, disappointed sound. Christmas is always a little sad, after such busy preparations. The unwanted trees lay on the stone floor, watching the furnace light flicker on a hatchet that had been left there.

The day after Christmas a man came in who wanted some green boughs to decorate a cemetery. The grocer took the hatchet, and seized the trees without ceremony. They were too disheartened to care. Chop, chop, chop, went the blade, and the sweet-smelling branches were carried away. The naked trunks were thrown into a corner.

And now our tree, what was left of him, had plenty of time to think. He no longer could feel anything, for trees feel with their branches, but they think with their trunks. What did he think about as he grew dry and stiff? He thought that it had been silly of him to imagine such a fine, gay career for himself, and he was sorry for other young trees, still growing in the fresh hilly country, who were enjoying the same fantastic dreams.

Now perhaps you don't know what happens to the trunks of leftover Christmas trees. You could never guess. Farmers come in from the suburbs and buy them at five cents each for bean poles and grape arbors. So perhaps (here begins the encouraging part of this story) they are really happier, in the end, than the trees that get trimmed for Santa Claus. They go back into the fresh moist earth of spring, and when the sun grows hot the quick tendrils of the vines climb up them and presently they are decorated with the red blossoms of the bean or the little blue globes of the grape, just as pretty as any Christmas trinkets.

So one day the naked, dusty fir poles were taken out of the cellar, and thrown into a truck with many others, and made a rattling journey out into the land. The farmer unloaded them in his yard and was stacking them up by the barn when his wife came out to watch him.

"There!" she said. "That's just what I want, a nice long pole with a fork in it. Jim, put that one over there to hold up the clothesline." It was the first time that anyone had praised our tree, and his dried-up heart swelled with a tingle of forgotten sap. They put him near one end of the clothesline, with his stump close to a flower bed. The fork that had been despised for a Christmas star was just the thing to hold up a clothesline. It was, and soon the farmer's wife began bringing out wet garments to swing and freshen in the clean bright air. And the very first thing that hung near the top of the Christmas pole was a cluster of children's stockings.

That isn't quite the end of the story, as the old fir trees whisper it in the breeze. The Tree That Didn't Get Trimmed was so cheerful watching the stockings, and other gay little clothes that plumped out in the wind just as though waiting to be spanked, that he didn't notice what was going on — or going up — below him. A vine had caught hold of his trunk and was steadily twisting upward. And one morning, when the farmer's wife came out intending to shift him, she stopped and exclaimed. "Why, I mustn't move this pole," she said. "The morning glory has run right up it." So it had, and our bare pole was blue and crimson with color.

Something nice, the old firs believe, always happens to the trees that don't get trimmed. They even believe that someday one of the Christmas-tree bean poles will be the starting point for another Magic Beanstalk, as in the fairy tale of the boy who climbed up the bean tree and killed the giant. When that happens, fairy tales will begin all over again.

CONTRIBUTORS

FRANK SULLIVAN (1892-1976) was a lively member of that uniquely American breed of journalists — the urbane observer of the urban — the humorous newspaperman. Every day for nearly three decades, his loyal readership turned to his column in *The New York World* to enjoy his comic gift for transforming a simple news item into an absurdist fantasy. The annual appearance of his Christmas poem in the *New Yorker* magazine marked the start of the holiday season all around the town. "Crisp New Bills For Mr. Teagle" was published in 1935.

WILLA CATHER (1875-1947) wrote truthfully, simply, and with great skill about her frontier childhood, growing up on the unsettled plains of Nebraska. Her coming-of-age novel, *My Antonia,* records this bygone era with honesty and richness of detail. As the last century drew to a close, Ms. Cather's pioneer spirit carried her East to New York City where she began to write short stories for *McClure's* magazine. "The Burglar's Christmas," published in 1896, is a charming example of one such story.

BUDD SCHULBERG (1914-) spent his early years surrounded by the glitter of Hollywood's glamorous film colony. His father, B. P. Schulberg, was the legendary producer and studio chief at Paramount Pictures. With his firsthand knowledge of the go-go world of entertainment, Mr. Schulberg wrote *What Makes Sammy Run, The Harder They Fall,* and *The Disenchanted.* "My Christmas Carol," published in 1953, is a kid's-eye view of Christmas at the top.

DAMON RUNYON (1884-1946), American journalist and playwright, is renowned for his marvelous short stories. Written in New Yorkese, littered with streetwise insights, and washed down with a slice of cheesecake from Mindy's, best-loved tales of the city such as "Guys and Dolls," "Little Miss Marker," "Butch Minds The Baby," and "Baseball Hattie" lit the literary landscape like a marquee on Broadway's Great White Way. "Dancing Dan's Christmas" was published circa 1930.

O. HENRY (1862-1910), the pseudonym for William Sydney Porter, was forced to adopt his nom de plume to write the first of hundreds of short stories from a prison cell in Ohio Federal Prison. Scores of writers have tried to imitate his trademark style for surprising or shocking the reader with a trick ending, but few come close to duplicating his wondrous imagination — Mr. Porter was a natural. "The Gift of the Magi" was published in 1906.

JAMES THURBER (1894-1961) was a charter member of that college-educated coterie of diners that broke their bread around the Algonquin round table. He began his career as a *New Yorker* cartoonist and used this skill to decorate many of his stories with hilarious illustrations that became the Thurber trademark. Often compared to Mark Twain, for his peculiarly biting wit, he claimed never to have read a word by that illustrious gentleman of letters. "The Secret Life of Walter Mitty," "The Male Animal," and "My Life and Hard Times" are his best-known works. "Merry Christmas" was published in 1936.

CHRISTOPHER MORLEY (1890-1957) was a superb editor, beginning his publishing career at Doubleday, Page & Company in 1913. Over a long and celebrated career, he wrote columns for *The Saturday Evening Post, Ladies' Home Journal,* was a founder of *The Saturday Review* and a Book-of-the-Month Club judge. In his spare time, Mr. Morley penned essays, short stories, poetry, plays, and novels. "The Christmas Tree That Didn't Get Trimmed" was published in 1919.